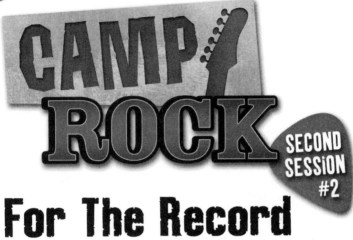

For The Record

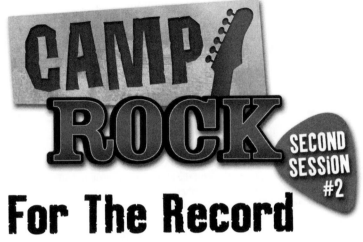

For The Record

By Lucy Ruggles

Based on "Camp Rock," Written by Karin Gist & Regina Hicks and Julie Brown & Paul Brown

New York

visit us at www.abdopublishing.com

Reinforced library bound edition published in 2010 by Spotlight, a division of ABDO Group, 8000 West 78th Street, Edina, Minnesota 55439. This edition reprinted by arrangement with Disney Press, an imprint of Disney Book Group, LLC. www.disneybooks.com

Library of Congress Cataloging-in-Publication Data

Ruggles, Lucy.
  Camp Rock second session / adapted by Lucy Ruggles ; based on "Camp Rock," written by Karin Gist ... [et al.]. -- Reinforced library bound ed.
     p. cm.
  ISBN 978-1-59961-541-7 (v. 1) -- ISBN 978-1-59961-542-4 (v. 2) -- ISBN 978-1-59961-543-1 (v. 3) -- ISBN 978-1-59961-544-8 (v. 4)
  I. Gist, Karin. II. Camp Rock (Motion picture) III. Title.
PZ7.R8859Cam 2010
[Fic]--dc22
                                        2009002938

All Spotlight books have reinforced library binding and are manufactured in the United States of America.

CHAPTER ONE

"Now for the secret ingredient," Mitchie Torres said triumphantly as she dumped a bag of confectioners' sugar into the jumbo bowl in front of her. Some of the white powder wafted back into the air and settled on her head, making her brown hair appear streaked with gray.

But Mitchie didn't care. She was helping her mother, Connie Torres, bake up a batch of brownies, and she was in a good mood—

a fabulous mood, actually. And why shouldn't she be? The sun was shining, the campers were singing, the familiar faces were all there (plus a few new ones), and it was another beautiful morning at Camp Rock.

"That makes three of us in the entire world who know the secret ingredient to Connie's Baritone Brownies," Mitchie said, brushing sugar from her hands and smiling at her mother. "You, me, and now Caitlyn."

"Just three?" Connie asked as she placed the spinning blades of a mixer into the chocolate batter. A smile crossed her face. "You mean you haven't told Shane?"

Mitchie's friend and cabinmate, Caitlyn Gellar, was standing next to her at the kitchen counter. She laughed as her friend's face turned bright red.

Caitlyn's days of working in the kitchen as punishment for last session's food fight with Tess Tyler were over, but she still liked to hang out with Mitchie and Connie.

Sometimes she even brought her laptop along to let them preview her latest musical creation.

"Is that what you think of me?" Mitchie asked, playing along with her mom. "That I'd reveal something as top secret as your brownie recipe to the first pop star to become my friend?"

True, Mitchie and Shane Gray had shared a fantastic moment the night of Final Jam when they had sung together in front of everyone. But even though she wanted to tell him about silly things like her mom's brownie recipe, there just wasn't enough time! Now that Camp Rock's Second Session was in full swing, her days were packed with jams, classes, singing, and dancing with all her new friends.

Still, she thought, Shane Gray! I can't believe I'm friends with one of the members of Connect Three—one of the biggest bands ever! It feels like a dream. . . .

Connie laughed, breaking into Mitchie's reverie. "Of course not, but I'm afraid there are more than three in the brownie 'know.' I told your father."

"Mrs. Torres!" Caitlyn exclaimed. "Loose lips sink ships!"

Their conversation was interrupted by the entrance of Camp Rock's director, Brown Cesario.

"Hello, Masters of the Mess Hall of Fame," Brown said as he came into the kitchen.

"Don't you mean *Mistresses* of the Mess Hall of Fame?" corrected Mitchie.

Brown nodded. "Of course," he agreed. "Ooh, brownies!" He dipped his finger into the rich, fudgy batter.

Connie swatted him away. "Brown, keep your hands out of my Baritone Brownies," she chided.

"Named after me, I'm sure." He winked. "Sorry. Can't help myself. This day just keeps getting better and better."

"Why's that?" Caitlyn asked.

Brown looked thoughtful, as if weighing whether or not he should tell them. But he quickly cracked. "I just heard that my old friend Rex Riley is dropping in tomorrow for a surprise visit."

Caitlyn's eyes nearly popped out of her head. "You mean, *the* Rex Riley?" she asked, astonished.

Brown nodded. "That's the one. I haven't seen him since I was touring with Guns N' Roses—they were opening for Aerosmith— and he was just getting started, doing some promotion for INXS," he said wistfully. For a moment he gazed off into space, as if remembering something from long, long ago.

Caitlyn was speechless. "Wow," she finally managed to say.

But Connie and Mitchie just looked at each other in confusion. Neither of them had any clue who Rex Riley was, or why his visit would cause the normally chatty Caitlyn to be rendered mute.

Caitlyn noticed their blank expressions. "Rex Riley," she repeated matter-of-factly, hoping to ring a bell. Nothing. Still blank. "The world-famous music producer and record executive who just happened to launch the career of almost every major musical talent of this millennium?" she continued.

"Oooh," mother and daughter both said, nodding their heads as if they understood.

Caitlyn eyed them. "You still don't know who we're talking about, do you?"

"Nope." Mitchie shrugged, shaking her head.

"Shelby, The Brooklyn Brothers, Alyssa Sharp . . . Jordan Davids?" Caitlyn persevered, listing the names of just a few of the pop stars and bands Rex Riley had personally ushered into fame and fortune.

Those names finally got Mitchie's attention. She had heard of all them—and listened to a few, including Jordan Davids. He was one of the biggest singers in the business right now—and one of Connect Three's biggest competitors on the charts. This meant he was also Shane's competition. Mitchie felt a thread of worry weave its way into her growing excitement.

Caitlyn, however, didn't seem concerned at all. "Wait till everyone hears about this!" she exclaimed, jumping up and down in the middle of the kitchen.

"Hold your horses," Brown said, raising his hands. "Let's keep this quiet until Rex gets here. You remember how much excitement Shane and Connect Three's visit created last session. I don't want to cause a commotion just yet." Caitlyn's face fell slightly.

"Can you promise me that?" Brown went on, looking between Mitchie and Caitlyn.

The two girls nodded. "We promise," they said together.

"You, too," Brown said, eyeing Connie.

"Caterer's honor," she said, holding up her spatula in a mock salute.

"Good," Brown said, satisfied that news of his famous friend's impending visit would not leave the four walls of the kitchen. "Carry on, then." Dipping his finger one more time into the batter, he rushed out before Connie could swat at him again.

"Wow," Caitlyn murmured after Brown left. "Rex Riley. That's something."

"Sure is," Mitchie agreed, already wishing she hadn't had to promise she wouldn't tell. Shane would want to know that the man behind his biggest competitor would soon be sharing the Camp Rock grounds.

Tess Tyler looked at herself in the cabin mirror, searching for her best angle. She turned left, then right, tilted her chin down, then up. Still not satisfied, she pouted in the mirror, opening her blue eyes wide.

Behind her, Lorraine Burgess, the newest member of Tess's entourage, was doing vocal warm-ups with Ella.

Like Mitchie, Tess had returned for Second Session, along with her cabinmates, Ella and

Peggy. But ever since Peggy had gone solo at Final Jam—and won—things had been a bit tense. Having Lorraine bunk with them for this session had helped . . . a little.

"Maggie made me mash my M&M's . . . mmm, mmm . . . Maggie made me mash my M&M's . . . mmm, mmm . . ." Ella sang each verse higher, humming in between to perfect her pitch.

"How *coool* is the pool? How *coool* is the pool?" Lorraine sang over her, drawing her lips into an exaggerated *O*.

Tess rolled her eyes in the mirror. "Jeez!" she snapped, turning to face Ella and Lorraine. "Can't a girl get a moment's silence around here? *How coool is the poool. Mitchie made me mash my M&M's,*" she sang in imitation. "Enough already!"

"It's Maggie, actually," Lorraine corrected quietly, her cheeks flushing beneath her red hair.

Tess winced and brought her hand to her

head. "Whatever. I need to focus, and I can't with you two chanting your warm-ups all the time." She flopped down on the designer quilt spread atop her bunk.

"Sorry," Ella replied. "But our voice coach told us we needed to exercise our vocal cords. And this is our only free time."

"Well, I need to exercise my need to get out of these woods and on to the pop charts," Tess said impatiently. "No offense, girls, but I am destined for greatness, and there's no way a record producer is going to recognize my potential if I'm not getting my voice out there. I mean, jams are fun and all, but they're not *real* performances."

Tess looked intently at Lorraine, who quickly nodded her red, ponytailed head in affirmation. In the short time since she'd arrived at Camp Rock, Lorraine had fallen firmly under Tess's spell. Just as Mitchie, Caitlyn, and Peggy had before her. Luckily for Lorraine, since Final Jam Tess had been showing her softer side—occasionally.

"Ever since I was a little girl," Tess continued, "my mom knew I was gonna be huge one day. I mean, of course—I'm T.J. Tyler's daughter! But bigger than her, even. And Camp Rock is just a stepping-stone. So I say, let's get this show on the road!"

Tess grabbed her pillow from the bed and scrunched it under her chin. She bit a manicured fingernail and squinted, deep in thought. "But how?" she wondered aloud.

Lorraine perched on Tess's bed beside her. She folded her long legs under her and mirrored Tess's questioning face. "How?" she repeated pensively.

"Oh, yeah. How?" Ella added.

The question hung heavy in the hot, summer air.

CHAPTER TWO

After all the dance classes Mitchie had already taken at Camp Rock, she practaically felt like she could teach one. But that wasn't on the top of her to-do list. Luckily, Shane had enjoyed his time at Camp Rock so much (and his label had enjoyed the positive press), that he'd decided to stay. That meant Shane could continue to teach classes. Today he would be leading advanced hip-hop. Mitchie was excited to see him, but a little nervous. What if she let her secret about Rex's visit slip?

As she followed Caitlyn into the dance studio, Mitchie glanced around. No sign of Shane yet, but she did spot most of her friends. Peggy was there, as well as Lola Scott, Barron James, Sander Loya, Andy, and even Colby Miller—who had first come to Camp Rock for Second Session. After a rocky start (he'd almost had to go home until Mitchie helped him), Colby now looked quite comfortable in the studio.

Mitchie smiled as she also caught sight of Shane's Connect Three bandmates—and guest counselors for the day—Nate and Jason, who popped in periodically to run new songs by Shane and "help" him teach classes. The pop stars fit right in, which wasn't surprising. After all, the three band-mates had met at Camp Rock.

"Hey, Mitchie!" Nate called out cheerfully when he spotted her.

13

"Hey, yourself," Mitchie said, smiling.

"Hey," Caitlyn replied casually. She was one of the few girls at Camp Rock who didn't still go gaga over Connect Three's surprise appearances. She, for one, was more interested in pop producers than pop stars. She crossed the dance floor to stretch at the wooden bar set up in front of the wall-length mirrors.

"I better warm up, too," said Mitchie, going to join Caitlyn. "Hey," she whispered as she propped her leg on the dance bar next to Caitlyn and leaned forward. "Have you told anyone about Rex's visit?"

"No!" Caitlyn cried in exasperation, causing other campers to glance over at them. "And it's been *so* hard," Caitlyn continued, quieter this time. "Do you know how big of a deal this is? Rex Riley is, like, one of the hottest names in the record business today."

Mitchie sighed. "But we promised Brown."

Caitlyn considered this regretfully. "Yeah, yeah," she moaned. She sat down on the floor and crossed her legs. Mitchie followed.

"Do you think we—" Mitchie's sentence was interrupted by the appearance of Peggy, who sat down beside the girls on the shiny floor. Since stepping out of Tess's shadow, Peggy had gotten closer to Mitchie and Caitlyn. Now, seeing her friends' guilty expressions, she grew curious.

"Oh, my gosh, you're totally talking about something. What is it? You have to tell me!" she begged.

Caitlyn and Mitchie glanced at each other nervously.

"Nothing," Caitlyn said, shrugging. "We were just talking about this new move we're trying to pin down."

Peggy eyed her two friends suspiciously. "I don't buy that. Seriously, what are you talking about?"

Mitchie could see her friend cracking under the pressure. "It's Rex Riley!" Caitlyn cried, unable to contain herself any longer.

"He's coming to visit Camp Rock, but Brown doesn't want us to tell anyone."

Peggy's mouth fell open. "Rex Riley?" she repeated in awe. "Wow."

Just as the "wow" escaped her mouth, Shane came through the door of the dance studio. As always, he looked effortlessly cool, his shaggy brown hair falling across his eyes just so. Seeing Nate and Jason, Shane broke into a grin and crossed the dance floor to give each of them a welcoming clap on the back. He hadn't known his bandmates were dropping in for a visit.

"I thought you guys were laying tracks this week," Shane said, his dark eyes twinkling.

"We were," Nate said, rolling his eyes. "But Jason thinks we need to go up-tempo on track nine, and I think we need to go down. You need to make the final call."

Watching the boys in the mirror, Peggy turned back to Mitchie. "Have you told Shane yet?" she whispered.

"No," Mitchie lamented. "We promised Brown we wouldn't tell anyone."

Peggy nodded her head, understanding Mitchie's predicament. It was common knowledge to anyone who had heard of Rex that he and Shane didn't exactly see eye-to-eye. Shane would want to know that Rex was coming to Camp Rock. But Mitchie wasn't the kind of girl who broke her promises—even if Caitlyn couldn't stop herself.

"Well . . ." Peggy shrugged. "I guess he'll know soon enough! Secrets don't stay hidden for long around here." She shot a meaningful look at Mitchie.

Mitchie felt herself blush. Peggy had a point. At the beginning of the summer, she had told everyone her mom was a big TV executive. It was, of course, a total lie, but she had just wanted to fit in with Tess's crowd. But then Tess found out the truth and called her on it. It had been awful. Everyone had been so angry—including Shane. He had been especially hurt by Mitchie's lie. Luckily, her friends had forgiven her, and now things were looking up. Mitchie was determined to put all that behind her.

Just as she was about to respond to Peggy, Shane stepped to the front of the studio. "Hey, everyone. Looks like we've got some special guests today."

"Who?" Jason asked excitedly, spinning around to look for the guests.

Nate rolled his eyes.

"Um, you," explained Shane.

"Oooh." Jason nodded, grinning widely. "Right."

Shane shook his head in wonder. "I also see we have some old pros in this class." He smiled at Mitchie. "So why don't we just jump into a new routine I came up with?"

Behind Shane, Nate cleared his throat.

"Uh, I mean *we* came up with," Shane corrected himself, smiling back at Nate.

Shane, Nate, and Jason proceeded to teach

the routine's first sixteen counts. While Mitchie's body followed the choreography effortlessly, her thoughts were anything but smooth. By keeping her promise to Brown, did she risk hurting Shane all over again?

"Sweetie, could you please grab the spinach from the walk-in fridge?" Connie asked her daughter later that day.

Mitchie was sitting at the kitchen table, silently grating cheese for dinner. Her thoughts were still swirling. She got up and went to the fridge, but instead of spinach, she returned bearing a bunch of carrots by their green, leafy stems. Absentmindedly, she handed them to her mother, who looked at Mitchie strangely.

"Unless we're having carrot lasagna for lunch, I think you might have misheard me," Connie teased. Mitchie barely cracked a smile. "Honey," she said, growing concerned, "is everything okay?"

"Sure, Mom. I'm fine." Mitchie returned to the fridge, and this time she came back with a huge bag of spinach. "Can I ask you a question? Hypothetically, if you made a promise to someone, but keeping that promise meant you might hurt someone else, someone you cared about, would you break it?"

Connie raised one eyebrow. "Hypothetically?" she repeated. "I'd say, unless it put someone in grave danger, a promise is a promise. Hypothetically, of course."

"That's what I thought," Mitchie said with a sigh. "Hypothetically."

It looked like Shane would have to wait to find out about Rex's visit with the rest of Camp Rock.

Chapter Three

One of the things Mitchie loved most about camp were the cookouts. Brown liked to man the grill himself in a tattered red apron that read ROCK N' GRILL across the front. There was also something about a camp hot dog that tasted better than any other hot dog. Mitchie was pretty sure everyone at Camp Rock agreed.

But that night it wasn't the smell of hot dogs and burgers wafting over the barbecue area that had campers' mouths watering; it was the news of Rex's impending arrival. Word had gotten out. Everywhere, campers murmured excitedly about the music producer's surprise visit. "Have you heard? Why do you think he's coming? When is he supposed to get here?" campers whispered from ear to ear.

Busy flipping burgers, Brown was oblivious to the fact that his secret had been leaked. Unfortunately, Mitchie, who was bringing out the last bowl of potato chips from the kitchen, was oblivious, too.

At one of the picnic tables, Tess sat with Lorraine, Ella, and Peggy. Tess had managed to get the information out of Peggy. Now she was busy detailing her plan to grab the producer's attention and snag the record deal she had always dreamed of—and, of course, deserved. "Song Showcase is in a couple of days, right?" she asked, her eyes scanning the crowd.

Ella and Peggy nodded.

"What's Song Showcase?" asked Lorraine.

Tess looked at her impatiently. "Oh, yeah, you're new," she said flatly. "Ella, fill her in."

"There are a few of them throughout the session," Ella explained. "It's a chance for us to, like, showcase the latest songs we've been working on."

Lorraine nodded. That sounded cool. She wondered what outfit she could wear. Lorraine was an amazing designer and had lots of handmade clothes. She enjoyed showing them off.

"Anyway, as *I* was saying," Tess said, turning the conversation back to more important matters, "the showcase is coming up, and I bet Rex will be there. In fact, I'm sure that's why he's coming—to scout out new talent. That's how my mom was discovered. She was performing at an open-mike night and a producer saw her. The rest, as they say in the biz, is history."

"Does your mom know Rex?" Lorraine asked, her green eyes wide.

"Of course," Tess said, flicking a piece of hair behind her shoulder. "Everyone knows everyone in this industry. It's like a big club. My mom went to his huge Labor Day party in the Hamptons last summer. We got his holiday card this year, too. It was so cute! His dog was wearing those fake reindeer antlers." She held her fingers up to her head to demonstrate.

"Yeah, he and my mom are tight," Tess continued confidently. "She probably told him I'd be here this summer, and the showcase will be the perfect opportunity to show him what I can do. I mean, he's not gonna sign me just because I'm T.J. Tyler's daughter," she stated sternly. "I have to show him I'm star material."

"Do you have a new song, Tess?" Peggy asked out of curiosity. She hadn't heard Tess working on one.

"No," Tess snapped. "But I don't have to sing a brand new song. Rex won't know if the one I pick is one I've sung before. . . ." Her blue eyes started to look frantic.

"Sure," Peggy assured her, trying to keep Tess from freaking out. "You can sing whatever you want. I just thought maybe that was the point of the showcase, to sing new . . ." Her voice trailed off as the look on Tess's face grew downright icy.

"I have one that I've been working on," Lorraine offered. "I've been writing it since I got here. It's called, 'Ambition.' It's not perfect, but it's almost done." She shrugged. "You can sing that, Tess, if you want."

"Perfect!" Tess pounced on the idea. "Oh, and, if Rex decides to put it on the album, you'll even get a songwriting credit!"

Lorraine seemed pleased at the idea, but Peggy just rolled her eyes. Leave it to Tess to steal someone else's spotlight—before there was even a spotlight. Some things never changed. Peggy was about to excuse herself to get in line for one of the juicy hamburgers

Brown was cooking when Shane walked by.

Tess jumped up, her blonde hair bouncing. "Shane!" she cried, grabbing his arm. "You're exactly who I wanted to see."

Shane eyed Tess suspiciously. "Why's that?"

"I just wanted advice on how to impress Rex, and you've worked with all sorts of record execs before. Any words of wisdom on how to get his attention? You know, show him I'm ready for a record deal?"

Shane furrowed his brow. "Rex?" he repeated, puzzled.

"Rex Riley," Tess said. She slapped him lightly on the arm, as if he was teasing her by playing dumb. "He's coming here to visit. Everyone knows."

Shane's face grew pale. Tess suddenly realized that Shane wasn't playing. He *hadn't* heard about Rex's visit.

Shane glanced around, a confused, and increasingly angry, look on his face. Why did he always seem to be the last to know anything at Camp Rock? His gaze settled on Mitchie. She had just delivered a bowl of potato chips to the condiments table and was crossing the picnic area toward them. She smiled and waved.

"Hey," she said when she reached Tess and Shane. "What's up?"

"What's up is that Rex Riley is coming to Camp Rock," Shane answered, stone-faced.

"You know?" Mitchie asked, surprised and relieved. "That's great! I've been wanting to tell you, but—"

Shane cut her off. "But *you* didn't," he said angrily. "Tess did. How could you have kept that from me when you knew it would be a big deal?"

Mitchie looked back and forth between Tess and Shane, her heart racing. "Tess, how did you know? It was supposed to be a secret."

Tess smirked. "Not a well-kept one, I guess. Everyone's talking about it!"

Their conversation was interrupted by the

sound of a loud cowbell. The camp music director, Dee La Duke, was happily banging away on it with a drumstick. Standing next to her on the lakeside stage, Brown—oven mitts still on his hands—covered his ears.

"Thank you, Dee," he said when she finally stopped. "I think we've got the attention of every camper *and* cow in a thirty-mile radius." Dee smiled, and Brown turned to face the crowd. "Well, mates, before we eat," he said, looking more like a suburban dad and less like a onetime rock star in his apron and chef's hat, "I'd like to make an announcement. This week, Camp Rock will be lucky to have a very special visitor." Excitement rippled through the crowd, even though almost everyone knew what was coming. "My friend, and the executive producer at Sweet Jam Records, Rex Riley."

Campers burst out into hoots and applause. "Some of you may know his work," he shouted over their cries. "Rex discovered a number of today's biggest talents, including Camp Rock's own Jordan Davids."

Some of the girls screamed, and Lola let out a loud catcall, causing everyone to laugh. Everyone except for Shane, who stood red-faced next to Mitchie. She wanted to explain why she hadn't been able to tell him about Rex's visit earlier.

"Shane," Mitchie said over the rising din, "I wasn't trying to hide it from you. I just promised—"

Again, he cut her off. "Save it." He scowled. "I've heard your excuses before." Turning, he stormed off in the direction of his cabin.

Mitchie stood, openmouthed and confused. Sure, she could understand if Shane was upset that she'd kept a secret from him; but *this* upset? Why had he stormed off without letting her explain? Rex and Jordan were Shane's competitors on the charts, but it wasn't like it was the end of the world!

Every artist had to compete for his or her space on the billboard. Maybe there was something more going on. But the only way she would find out was if Shane talked to her—and she doubted that that was going to happen anytime soon.

Caitlyn, seeing Shane storm off, made her way over to Mitchie's side. "What was that about?" she asked her friend.

"I have no idea," Mitchie said, shrugging her shoulders.

Meanwhile, up on the stage, Brown was still trying to talk over the chatter. "So let's make sure to give Rex a big Camp Rock welcome and make the next few performances your strongest ones yet. Now chow down!"

Once again, Dee clanged the dinner bell, and the campers turned their attention to the food.

Mitchie turned and gave Caitlyn a worried look. "I think I might have messed up."

CHAPTER FOUR

Shane had locked himself in his room in Brown's cabin and had not come out since the cookout the previous night. Mitchie knew this because she'd found an excuse to wander by the cabin half a dozen times, and each time she could hear him playing on his guitar. She had recognized one song. It was a new one he had shared with her a few days earlier at "their" spot—the bench by the hollowed-out tree. He had hinted that it was about her.

Mitchie smiled at the memory as she did another walk-by. But her smile quickly faded. That felt like so long ago. Shane had played the song while they sat enjoying the feel of the sun on their faces. It had been a great day. And now, the fear that she had ruined things with Shane for good was making her sick to her stomach.

Still, Mitchie couldn't understand why Shane had been *so* angry. It wasn't her fault, she reasoned, that Brown had made her promise to keep quiet. Plus, she had known Shane would find out eventually, just like everyone else. So it wasn't like she had intentionally hurt him. As she paced in front of Shane's cabin, Mitchie decided enough was enough. She had to know what was going on. She bounded up the wooden stairs and knocked on his door.

The strumming inside stopped, and Mitchie's heart pounded as she heard Shane's footsteps move toward the door. It cracked open to reveal him barefoot, wearing jeans and a faded concert T-shirt.

"Hey," he said, squinting in the sunlight.

"Hey," Mitchie said meekly. "Can I come in?"

"Sure." Shane opened the door further, stepping back into the cabin. He sat down in a chair, with the guitar in his lap. Mitchie perched uneasily on the edge of another chair. An awkward silence filled the room. "Mitchie . . ." he started.

"Shane . . ." Mitchie said at the same time, causing the tension to break. Both of them burst into laughter.

"Ladies first," he said, when he stopped laughing.

Mitchie clasped and unclasped her hands in her lap. "I just wanted to say that I'm so sorry for not telling you about Rex's visit. Brown told my mom, Caitlyn, and me, but he made us *promise* not to tell anyone else. I wanted to tell you so badly because I thought you should know, but I didn't want to break my word. And then you were so angry yesterday at the cookout. I didn't understand why. . . ."

Shane smiled, almost sadly. He took a deep breath. "I know." He sighed. "I forgive you for not telling me. You did the right thing."

"You do?" Mitchie said, relieved. Then she cocked her head. "Wait, I did?"

"Of course." Shane gently set his guitar on the floor. "A promise is a promise. I wasn't really mad at you. I was just upset because, well, there's kind of bad blood between Rex and me."

"I know he's Jordan's producer, which makes him the competition in a way," Mitchie observed. "But don't you deal with that all the time? I don't mean to be insensitive, Shane, but it's business, not personal, right?"

Shane grimaced. "Actually," he said, "it *is* personal. You know how Brown said Jordan was one of 'Camp Rock's own'?"

Mitchie nodded. "Yeah. I hadn't known that till yesterday."

Shane stood up and began to pace back and forth across the cabin's creaky floorboards. "Well, he was also my bunkmate and best friend . . . until Rex got to him. We did everything together: played basketball, wrote songs, sang together. Then Rex came to camp to scope out his next 'project' and chose Jordan—over me."

"I can see how that would be disappointing," sympathized Mitchie. "But it didn't stop you from having your own success, right?"

"I wouldn't have cared about it all," Shane said, turning to face her, "if that were the end of it. But Rex changed Jordan. All of a sudden, my best friend, the most laid-back person in the world, who loved to climb trees and play the guitar, became this spoiled pop star. He thought he was better than everyone else, including me."

"Sounds like someone else I know,"

Mitchie said, trying to sound lighthearted.

Shane nodded. He knew Mitchie was referring to his old attitude. "Rex turned him into this commercial product. Jordan totally lost his sound. At first, we would fight about it—that is, when he remembered to write or call." Shane paused, as if reliving the memories.

He went on. "Then we just stopped talking altogether. Things only got worse when I got into the business. The magazines created this whole feud between us—which I guess wasn't so far off base—and blew it way out of proportion. By the time I realized it was all so silly, it was too late. Anyway, I blame Rex. He loved the attention—good or bad. And Rex never tried to patch things up. As long as Jordan's records kept selling he was happy. So, this is why I'm not really looking forward to his visit."

"Shane," Mitchie said, sympathetically, "I'm so sorry. That's horrible. If I had known . . ."

". . . You would have told me. I know. All I can do is grin and bear it, I guess." Shane forced a smile.

"Well," Mitchie said, thinking, "maybe there's a bright side. Brown obviously likes Rex, and he's usually a good judge of character. Is it possible that he's changed? Or that he wasn't as bad as you thought?"

"Maybe," said Shane. Then he shook his head. "Doubtful."

"And," Mitchie said, smiling, "maybe he's visiting for business as well as pleasure. Maybe his next big star is right here at Camp Rock!"

"Unfortunately," said Shane, "I wouldn't be surprised if that was exactly his plan. I just hope Rex picks someone who knows how to stay true to the music. . . ."

CHAPTER FIVE

Caitlyn ran her fingers along the wall as she walked down the hall that led to one of the room's in Keynote—the rehearsal cabin. On her shoulder was a black satchel containing her laptop. With Rex set to arrive anytime now, she knew she had to get to work producing a music sample. And not just any old sample but the most kickin' sample she had ever produced, one that summed her up and captured her passion and soul and love for music on one round, shiny disc. Easier said than done, she thought.

Hearing something, or rather someone, as she neared the door that opened into the room, Caitlyn stopped and listened. She couldn't see the girl, but she recognized the voice. It was Tess.

"*I know I've got it in me; That fire, the desire,*" Tess sang.

Tess has improved since last session, Caitlyn couldn't help but think.

And Tess had. She was more real. She didn't hide her voice behind all the fancy vocal pyrotechnics.

Caitlyn peeked her head through the open door. Tess was standing in front of the grand piano, her back to the door. Caitlyn stepped into the room and leaned against the wall to listen quietly.

"*I've got the ambition; Don't need your superstition; Gonna make it on my own.*" Tess struggled with the final note, trying to hit it several times, but with each attempt her voice quavered and she finally gave up.

"Darn it! Tess, you can do this," she said, talking to herself. "You *have* to do this to impress Rex. This might be your one shot at a record deal. You can't blow it. Think how embarrassed your mom would be to have a daughter who couldn't even hit a stupid high note."

Tess plopped down onto the piano bench, her back still to the door. Then she slumped over, obviously distressed. Caitlyn was afraid Tess might start to cry. Clearing her throat, Caitlyn pretended to have just walked in the door.

"Hey, Tess," Caitlyn said, trying to sound nonchalant.

Tess spun around, startled. "Caitlyn!" she exclaimed. "How long have you been standing there?"

"I just walked in," she fibbed, biting her lip and setting her bag on top of the piano.

"Whatever," Tess said haughtily. "I'm just practicing for the showcase. I hear Rex will be there, and I have to make sure he gets the performance he expects. I'm sure my mom has already gotten him all worked up about seeing me perform." All traces of the vulnerability Caitlyn had just seen were gone.

"Sure. Right," Caitlyn replied skeptically. "I'm actually hoping to catch his attention, too. I would love to get an internship with his record label one day. That's why I'm down here—to work on a demo. Do you mind if I do that while you practice?" She had already started to unpack her laptop. Soon enough, a funky techno song was playing from the speakers.

Tess did not look pleased, but she nodded. "I was just leaving anyway."

Grabbing her purse and the sheet music she had been practicing from, Tess headed out of the room. At the door, she stopped and turned. "Hey, Caitlyn?" she added.

"Yeah?" Caitlyn asked, looking up from her computer.

"Just don't get your hopes up. I mean about Rex. He's the real deal."

Caitlyn glared at Tess. Same old Tess, she thought. "Thanks," she replied sarcastically. "I'll keep that in mind."

Tess offered a prim smile and walked out, leaving Caitlyn to prove her wrong.

A hand reached up and tapped on the dark glass. "Please take a left here, Humphrey."

"Yes sir, Mr. Riley," replied Humphrey. The chauffeur swung the long, white limo past the Camp Rock sign.

"Ahhh," Rex sighed from the backseat, taking a sip from his crystal tumbler of sparkling water. "It's good to be back, surrounded by so much talent, so much . . . sound. I remember when I was a kid, Humphrey, how purely I loved the music!"

Rex marveled, thinking back to all those years ago when he had been a broke, long-haired boy, following the bands he loved with his old friend, Brown Cesario.

"Yes, sir, Mr. Riley," said Humphrey. "Those sound like good times."

"Humphrey," Rex said, leaning forward to talk through the divider. "I know the limo service told you to call me Mr. Riley, but please. It's been four years. Enough with the 'sir' stuff. Call me Rex."

"Yes, sir, Rex," replied Humphrey.

Rex sighed again and sank back into the black leather seat. Outside the tinted windows, campers had arranged "impromptu" practice sessions. As the limo eased to a stop, an a capella group seemed to form magically behind Brown, who had come to welcome his old friend.

"Brownie!" Rex called heartily, stepping out of the car almost before it stopped moving. He pulled Brown in for a bear hug.

"How you doin', mate?" asked Brown, grinning. "Holding up out there in that rat race they call the music industry, old man?"

Rex laughed at the friendly jibe. He knew he didn't look like an old man. He was in great shape—tall, trim, and dashing in an impeccably tailored suit and designer shoes that probably cost more than enrollment at Camp Rock. "What do you mean?" Rex said, pretending to be offended. "Age is a state of mind!"

Behind Rex, Barron and Sander launched into a reggaeton number. Brown shot them a look. "Barron, Sander, maybe you'd like to take Rex's luggage to the guest cabin?" he asked. It was more of a command than a question.

The boys nodded eagerly and sprang to the limo, where Humphrey was unloading Rex's bags.

Brown led Rex toward the center of the campgrounds. "How about a tour? A lot's changed since the last time you were here."

"I think last time I was here, you were sleeping in tents and singing into hairbrushes," Rex said smiling.

"Well, not quite." Brown laughed. "But we are proud of our improvements. Let me show you some of our state-of-the-art recording facilities."

Rex seemed to hesitate for a second, then reconsidered. "Great!"

The two of them walked toward the path that led to the recording studio, but they didn't get far. They stumbled upon a country crooner who had "coincidentally" chosen to sing his heart out on the very same path. Politely, Brown and Rex sidestepped him.

Only it didn't stop there. Brown was showing Rex all the new equipment in the control room, when the lights suddenly went up on a punk trio in the sound booth. They began jamming on their electric guitars. Brown shooed them out, apologizing to his friend. Rex was fine with it—until, outside the dance studio minutes later, a would-be pop princess nearly pierced their eardrums with her rendition of a Mariah Carey classic.

"You know," Rex said, cringing at the girl's shrill squawking, "what I really want to see is the mess hall. I've barely eaten anything since sushi last night with Beyoncé."

"Great idea," said a relieved Brown. "And wait till you try Connie's cooking. It's fantastic. . . . Beyoncé, you said?"

"Yeah." Rex sighed as he polished his designer sunglasses with his silk tie. "It's a hard-knock life."

"**M**ail call!" Dee's voice cried out happily as she approached the Vibe Cabin.

Ella, Tess, and Lorraine all perked up on their beds as Dee stepped through the door with her bulging mailbag. Peggy's bed was empty—she was off waiting with the other campers for Rex to arrive.

"Phew!" Dee exclaimed, slightly out of

breath. "You'd think your parents had shipped you off for the rest of your young-adult lives with all the stuff they send you!"

She pulled out a huge box wrapped in brown paper and delivered it into a beaming Ella's hands. "*Another* one for you, Ella. Lorraine, a few letters . . ." She handed over an inch-thick stack of letters. "And Tess . . ." Tess's eyes lit up. "Your mom sent an e-mail for you through Brown."

"Oh," Tess said, disappointed. Dee handed her a single piece of paper printed with the words, CAN'T WAIT TO TOUR WITH YOU THIS FALL! XOXO, T.J. Then she left to finish her mail rounds.

Ella read the e-mail over Tess's shoulder. "You call your mom T.J.?" she asked, scrunching her nose.

"Of course," Tess responded curtly. "We decided I'm way too old to call her 'Mom.' It's so babyish."

"*So* babyish," Lorraine confirmed, hiding

her own stack of letters behind her back. All of them were signed "Mom." "So, you're going to tour with your mom?" she asked, hoping to change the subject.

Tess nodded and began to talk about all the places she was going to go. As she did so, Lorraine stuffed her letters under her pillow. She could read them later when there was some more privacy. "Whoa," she said, when Tess paused. "That's so cool!"

Tess smiled, crossing the cabin to take her brush from the dresser. She then stood before the mirror, combing her long hair. It seemed to Tess that it had gotten blonder over the summer. She might not even need a trip to her mother's stylist for highlights in September.

"We're gonna have such an amazing time," Tess mused, "seeing the world and staying at all the best hotels, eating at the best restaurants, playing the biggest venues. Do you know what it's like to stand in front of three hundred thousand people screaming your name?"

Ella thought about this for a second. "No. Do you?"

"Well, no," Tess said quickly, "but it's almost the same when it's your mom's name and you're, like, right backstage. Besides, I'll know soon enough, once Rex gets here and discovers me."

"Rex!" Peggy cried, arriving breathlessly at the cabin door. "He's here! He just pulled in. Brown is giving him a tour."

Lorraine bounced up and down on the bed. "He's here! He's here!" Ella chanted.

"Tess," Lorraine said breathlessly, "why don't you go find him and say hello?"

Peggy saw a look of fear cross Tess's face. "He's at the mess hall with Brown now," she said quickly, coming to Tess's rescue. "But I'm sure he'll be at Eighties Night Jam tonight."

"Of course," said Tess. "I wouldn't want to

seem overeager. And it's not as if I can just run up to him looking like this and shake his hand! He has to get the full effect. If Rex is going to recognize me as his next big star, I'm going to have to look the part when I see him . . . again."

"How are you going to do that?" asked Lorraine.

Tess looked herself up and down in the full-length mirror, examining her short denim skirt, flip-flops, and designer T-shirt. "First of all," she said, tugging at the frayed bottom of the skirt, "a wardrobe change."

"Wardrobe change!" Lorraine clapped happily. This was her favorite part of being a performer. If her musical career didn't work out, she figured she could always go into costume design. In fact, she'd brought two entire trunks to camp just for the costumes that she lovingly designed and sewed at home. There wasn't enough room in the Vibe Cabin with all of the girls' stuff, so the trunks had had to be stored in an empty cabin.

"Lorraine," Tess demanded, "let's go look in your wardrobe trunks. I think I saw something *perfect* for my performance at the jam tonight."

Giddy with the attention, Lorraine hopped up, grabbed Tess's hand, and bounded out the cabin door.

CHAPTER SIX

"**B**ye, Mrs. Torres. See ya, Mitchie!" Shane called as he pushed open the back door of the mess hall and ran smack into a large figure in a dark suit. He stepped back. "Rex," he said through a set jaw.

"Shane," Rex acknowledged politely. "Long time, no see."

"Not long enough," Shane said under his breath.

"Shane, you remember my old friend, Rex Riley," his uncle said, coming up the stairs behind Rex.

"Sure, Uncle Brown," said Shane, his hands balled into fists. "He's hard to forget."

"Congratulations on Connect Three's last record, Shane. It's showing in the top ten this week."

"Yeah," Shane said curtly. "It is." Then, shooting Brown a loaded look, he excused himself.

"Well," Rex said after Shane had walked toward the dance studio.

"Well," Brown repeated, not sure how to handle the awkward exchange he had just witnessed between his nephew and his friend.

"Looks like Shane sure has grown up."

Brown smiled in relief. "You know, he really has. I think being back here has helped him get his head on straight. So, shall we get you that lunch?"

"We shall," said Rex as he followed Brown into the kitchen.

They walked into the mess hall to find Mitchie and her mother covered in white powder. A thin film of it covered the floor. On the counter were a large mixing bowl and a ten-pound bag of flour with half of its contents spilled out. As Rex and Brown swung through the door, Mitchie and Connie turned like two deer caught in the headlights or, more precisely, two people caught in a food fight.

"Cake," said Connie, by way of explanation.

"Cake?" repeated Brown.

"Cake," said Mitchie this time.

"My favorite," said a grinning Rex, unfazed. "What kind?" He glanced into the mixing bowl on the counter. "Obviously not flourless chocolate."

"No," said Connie, sheepishly wiping the flour from her face with her apron. "Strawberry. I'm Connie Torres." She held out her flour-covered hand.

"Pleasure to meet you, Connie," Rex said, shaking her hand. "I've heard so much about you. Brown won't stop raving about your catering."

Connie blushed. "You must be Rex."

"Indeed, I am," he answered.

"And this," said Brown, patting Mitchie on the back, "is Mitchie Torres. Connie's daughter, sous chef, and a mighty fine singer to boot."

Now it was Mitchie's turn to blush. "Nice to meet you, Mr. Riley."

"Mr. Riley?" Rex laughed. "If you call me that, I'll be looking around for my father! Please, call me Rex."

"So," Brown said, rubbing his hands together enthusiastically, "what's for lunch?"

"Well, let's see. Tomato gazpacho, bow-tie pasta salad with peppers and green peas, tarragon chicken salad, brioche rolls, and strawberry cake if you've saved room. It's a little simple, I'm afraid," Connie apologized to Rex, "but Brown didn't specify when you were arriving."

"Not at all!" Rex objected. "Sounds delicious. My stomach's already rumbling." Suddenly the phone in Rex's jacket started ringing to the tune of Jordan Davids' latest hit song. "Please excuse me," he said. "I have to take this. . . . Hello . . . Jordan! Hey, man. What's going on?"

Rex smiled at Connie and Mitchie. Then he stepped into the dining room for some privacy.

Mitchie and Connie exchanged impressed looks and continued chatting with Brown. None of them saw Caitlyn peek her head in the door by the pantry. Silently, she checked out the scene. There were Mitchie, Connie, and Brown. And there was Rex! Omigosh! she thought, suppressing an internal freak-out. And there was Rex's briefcase, right by the door. Caitlyn couldn't have planned it better herself!

Silently, Caitlyn placed a copy of her demo CD on top of the shiny leather briefcase. Then, just as quickly and quietly as she had come, she slipped away. She would have loved to meet Rex Riley right then and there, but she didn't want to arouse suspicion. She knew, after all, that Brown would strongly disapprove of campers bombarding Rex with their demos. Still, she wasn't taking her chances. In order to intern for Rex Riley, she would have to do some fancy footwork to impress him, and that began with getting him to listen to her work.

As Caitlyn came and went, unbeknownst to all in the kitchen, Rex's conversation with Jordan was heating up. Rex was pacing back and forth across the dining hall. When Brown poked his head in and shot him a quizzical look, Rex threw up his free hand and rolled his eyes. Something was obviously up with Jordan Davids.

"Um, excuse me, Connie, Mitchie," Brown

said, looking back at them. "I'm gonna let you finish up with your cake—or whatever you were doing—and check on Rex."

"No problem," said Mitchie as Brown exited to the dining room. She was curious to know what Rex and Jordan were talking about.

"So," Connie said quietly when Brown was gone, "Rex seems like a nice guy. He complimented my cooking. Can't argue with that!"

Mitchie glanced through the door into the room where Rex was now off the phone and in the midst of an intense conversation with Brown. "Yeah," Mitchie agreed. "He does seem like a nice guy." So, she thought, if he is such a good guy, how can Shane dislike him so much?

"**W**hat's going on?" Brown asked Rex. "Trouble in paradise?"

Rex let out a sarcastic laugh. "Ha! Paradise. Funny. You know Jordan's dating my other singer, Alyssa Sharp."

Brown nodded.

"Correction: *was* dating Alyssa Sharp. Apparently, she dumped him."

Brown winced. "Ouch. Been there."

"Haven't we all?" Rex sighed. "Anyway, that's not the worst part. The worst part is that now she's pulling out of the album they were supposed to record together. How do you like that?"

"Can you turn it into a solo album?" asked Brown.

"Maybe," replied Rex, shrugging. "Except now Jordan says he's too devastated to work, says there's no way he can even *think* about recording. He says it would remind him too much of her. This is a huge problem, as we wanted to get his next single out this fall." Rex shook his head and moaned.

Brown also shook his head. "Those creative music types," he said as they walked back into the kitchen. "I tell ya, they're hard to handle."

"*Very* hard to handle," said Rex.

"So sensitive," added Brown.

"Dramatic," agreed Rex.

Mitchie and Connie exchanged amused expressions at the irony of the men's conversation.

"Oh!" said Rex, remembering something. "There's a clipping I've been meaning to give you, an article about Stevie. You remember Stevie from back in the day?"

"Of course," said Brown. "Stevie Nicks," he explained for Connie and Mitchie's benefit.

Mitchie nodded, making an impressed face. Like the rest of the campers, she had become accustomed to Brown's tendency to name-drop.

"Hang on. It's in my briefcase." Rex bent down to retrieve the article from the briefcase. On top, he found a mysterious CD. "This must be yours," he said to Mitchie, setting it on the counter. He popped the clasps on his briefcase and pulled out a magazine clipping, which he handed to Brown. "Those were the days, weren't they, Brownie?" he said wistfully.

"Those were the days," Brown agreed, glancing down at the article.

As the two men went on a riff about the good old days, Connie and Mitchie smiled at each other. Brown and Rex were definitely two of a kind.

CHAPTER SEVEN

Just a few hours later, Camp Rock looked like it had been transported two decades back in time. Perhaps because Brown felt nostalgic with Rex around, he had gone all out for the Eighties Night Jam. With the help of Colby, Barron, and Sander, he'd hauled the karaoke machine, jam-packed with eighties hits, down to the stage by the lake.

Also inspired by Rex's visit—but for

different reasons—the campers had outdone themselves as well. The girls had crimped hair, and the boys wore puffy shorts—a la MC Hammer. They eagerly lined up to take the stage and cue their favorite eighties songs, bopping along to the music.

Tess, however, was patiently biding her time until Rex arrived. She didn't want to waste her stage time in front of just anybody. She had a plan, and Rex's presence was a key ingredient.

Finally he arrived and stood in the back of the crowd next to Brown. He was easy to pick out in his crisp designer suit and bright pink tie. Tess knew it was go-time. Grabbing her backup singers, Ella and Lorraine, Tess pushed her way to the front of the line at the karaoke table.

"Hey!" objected Lola, who was dressed in neon green leggings and an oversized white button-down shirt belted at the waist. "Not cool! I was up next!" she cried.

Ignoring Lola's protests, Tess leaned down on the table in front of Danny, the boy manning the karaoke machine. He also happened to have a huge, well-known crush on Tess.

"H-h-hi, Tess," Danny stammered nervously.

"Hi, Danny." Tess batted her eyelashes beneath her bright blue eye shadow. As always, she had gone overboard. In a ripped, black lace dress and matching gloves, a crimped nest of hair piled on top of her head, and a knot of fake pearls dangling from her neck, Tess was the spitting image of Madonna, the Early Years. "You know 'Like a Prayer'?" she asked.

"Sure I do," replied Danny.

"Great," she said as the last act came off the stage. "Hit it." Again, she grabbed Ella and Lorraine by the wrists and pulled them onto the stage. "All right, girls," she whispered as the intro music poured from the speakers, "don't screw it up." With that, she spun to face the audience and, more importantly, Rex.

Ella and Lorraine obediently began to "oooh" their way through the song's intro. Then Tess launched into the song, barely glancing at the TV monitor for word cues. From the crowd, Mitchie, Shane, Caitlyn, Peggy, and Colby watched.

"Wow," Peggy said, sounding genuinely surprised. "She's gotten better!"

Mitchie and Shane nodded their heads in agreement.

"Looks like her practicing has paid off," Caitlyn observed.

Mitchie looked over at Caitlyn quizzically. "What do you mean?"

"Oh," said Caitlyn, forgetting she was the only one who had seen Tess near tears in the rehearsal room the other morning. "I just mean I bet she's been practicing . . . to prepare for Rex, you know? She really wants to get his attention."

"Who doesn't?" asked Colby.

Shane rolled his eyes. "Anyone with any sense."

"That reminds me . . ." Caitlyn said. "I'll catch you guys in a few." Waving good-bye, she slipped off before anyone could ask where she was going.

Mitchie and Peggy looked at each other and shrugged before turning their attention back to Tess.

From up on the stage, Tess was still watching Rex intently. The only problem? He wasn't watching her.

Halfway through the first verse his phone had rung, and Rex had been chatting on it through the entire song. Tess danced, shimmied, and shook on the stage in her best impression of Madonna. But Rex was still talking energetically into his phone. Then he turned his back on her! *What does it take to get noticed around here?* Tess wanted to scream into the microphone. Instead, she faithfully sang the words crawling across the karaoke monitor until the final note.

Annoyed, Tess didn't bother to take a bow at the wild applause that followed her performance. Instead, Ella and Lorraine watched, puzzled, as she stormed off the stage.

"Tess, what's wrong?" Lorraine asked, hurrying after her. Concern spread across her face as she pulled her long red hair into a ponytail. "We did great—*you* did great!"

Tess's arms were crossed tightly across her chest. "He's *just like* my mother," she grumbled.

"Huh?" asked Lorraine, who couldn't understand Tess because her jaw was tightly clenched.

"Nothing. Look, Rex didn't even notice. He was too busy taking calls," Tess retorted.

"Maybe he was listening as he talked?" Lorraine was trying to sound positive. "You know, a lot of people can multitask, especially big executives."

Tess's jaw unclenched a little. "Yeah. Maybe," she allowed.

"Why don't you go talk to him and ask how he liked our performance? You said your mom is friends with him, right?"

"Right," Tess said uneasily.

"So what are you waiting for?" Lorraine asked.

Tess looked awkwardly between Lorraine and Rex, biting her bottom lip. "Okay," she said. "Why not? Great artists take chances, right?"

"Right." Lorraine nodded emphatically.

Tess made a determined beeline through the crowd toward Rex, who was tapping his foot along with the next song.

"Excuse me, excuse me," Tess repeated, pushing past campers as she zeroed in on Rex. Lorraine trailed behind her.

When she reached the two men, Tess planted herself confidently in front of them. "Hi, Brown," she said.

"Hello, Tess," Brown said, a bit startled to see her standing before him so suddenly.

Tess turned to Rex. "Hi, Rex."

Rex's eyebrow rose just slightly. "Um, hi . . ." He searched her face for a name. "I'm sorry. Do I know you?"

Tess began to shift nervously from foot to foot. "You don't remember? I'm Tess Tyler," she said, sticking out her hand. "T.J.'s daughter."

Rex shook it good-naturedly. "Oh, right!" he said, finally catching on. "Gosh. How is T.J.? It's been ages since we've seen each other! I forgot she had a daughter."

Tess's face turned bright red. He didn't remember her? How could he admit that? *In front of Lorraine!*

Suddenly, Rex's phone started ringing again. He glanced at the caller ID. "Jordan," he said through the side of his mouth to Brown. Looking back at Tess he said, "Excuse me. I have to take this." Turning his back on the group he began to speak in a hushed tone.

Seeing the disappointment in Tess's eyes,

Brown smiled encouragingly. "Tess, that was quite a performance!" he said.

"Thanks," she answered, halfheartedly. Then she turned to Lorraine. "Come on," she snarled. "Let's go." She was not going to be humiliated anymore.

"Bye, Brown!" Lorraine called over her shoulder as Tess dragged her back through the crowd.

Meanwhile, Caitlyn was enacting phase two of the Official Plan to Get Rex to Notice and One Day Hire Caitlyn Gellar, Future Music Producer to the Stars. As everyone else had been shamelessly following Rex around all day, hoping he'd catch a bit of their singing, Caitlyn had been doing reconnaissance. Rex had arrived in a white stretch limo that was currently parked in the camp lot. It was being watched by his chauffeur, and Caitlyn's new best friend, Humphrey.

As Peggy launched into her cover onstage

of a Donna Summers hit, Caitlyn made her way out to the parking lot.

"Hey, Humphrey!" she called out as she walked across the gravel.

Humphrey was leaning against the car door, eating his dinner, and enjoying the free concert. He smiled when he saw Caitlyn. She had introduced herself earlier and seemed like a nice girl.

"Hey, kiddo," said Humphrey, balling up a napkin and slam-dunking it into the bag on the hood of the car. "What are you doing out here? Shouldn't you be singing Michael Jackson or Cyndi Lauper or something over there?"

"Later," Caitlyn said. "But first, I brought you this." From her sweatshirt pocket, she produced a CD in a green jewel case and held it out to Humphrey.

"What's this?" he asked, taking the CD and turning it over in his hands. There was a homemade label pasted on the front.

"'Production Demo—Caitlyn Gellar,'" he read out loud. "Is this really you?"

"Sure is." Caitlyn beamed. "I made it today. It's a sample of the music I've produced this summer at camp. I was hoping you might be able to do me a favor and slip it into the CD player in Rex's limo," she said.

"Well, I don't know," Humphrey replied hesitantly. "Something like that could get me fired. You know how many people try to get Rex Riley to listen to their demos every year—man, every *day*? He's got crazies following him around, jumping over his fence, breaking into his car—*my* car."

"I know," said Caitlyn, "which is why I'm giving it to you and not breaking into your limo. 'Cause I'm not a crazy, see?"

Humphrey examined Caitlyn, dressed with eighties flair. He had to hand it to her—she had guts. "Okay, kid. You got it. I'll see what I can do."

"Really?" Caitlyn asked excitedly.

"Well, I can't make any promises," he said, holding up his hands.

Caitlyn smiled. "I know, I know. Thanks, Humphrey! You're the best." She gave him a friendly jab on the shoulder.

He laughed. "Watch out, kiddo. I'm not just Rex's driver; I'm also his bodyguard."

"Thanks again, Humphrey!" Caitlyn called as she walked back across the parking lot to rejoin the jam. "Mission accomplished," she whispered to herself, smiling.

Humphrey chuckled. He opened the car door and slid into the front seat, taking the disc from its case and inserting it into the CD player on the dashboard. As the music filled the front of the car, he nodded to the beat and tapped on the steering wheel. This was good! Not exactly his kind of music, but after working for Rex Riley for four years, he liked to think he knew a good sound when he heard it, and this was it. Unfortunately, while Humphrey might enjoy it, Rex, who usually sat behind the soundproof glass, wouldn't even hear it.

Back at the stage, it was finally Mitchie and Shane's turn. It had been Shane's idea to sign them up for a duet. After flipping through the encyclopedia-size book of songs, they had finally agreed on one: Joan Jett's version of "I Love Rock 'n Roll."

Shane and Mitchie smiled and laughed at each other as they sang. It was hard to be too serious when Shane wore a bright pink shirt under a white blazer and Mitchie was in a denim skirt over leggings with a ripped sweatshirt hanging off one shoulder. It was clear that they weren't just performing, they were having fun, and the entire camp sang along with the chorus, waving their hands in the air.

Toward the back of the crowd, Rex had his finger plugged into his ear so he could hear what Jordan was saying on the other line.

Looking up, he noticed Shane and Mitchie onstage.

"Hey, Jordan," Rex said, cutting his client off midsentence. "Let me call ya back, buddy. I think I got an idea."

He snapped the phone shut and turned to Brown, who was singing along with the campers. "Hey," Rex said, over the noise, "I didn't know Shane did duets."

"Sure does," said Brown, "if he has the right partner."

Rex smiled and nodded his head with the beat. "Hmm," he said to himself. He had an idea indeed.

CHAPTER EIGHT

Early the next morning, Connie heard a knock at the kitchen door. Thinking it was Mitchie, she called out, "Come on in! You're late, young lady!"

"I think that's the first time I've ever been called a 'young lady,'" a male voice said behind her.

Connie spun around, surprised to find Rex standing in the kitchen.

She laughed. "I'm sorry, Rex. I thought you

were Mitchie. She was supposed to be here ten minutes ago, and I've got two dozen quiches to get in the oven." She wiped her hands on her apron. "Are you looking for Brown?"

"Nope, I'm not looking for Brown," Rex said pleasantly. "May I?" he asked, gesturing to a chair at the table, which was covered with open cookbooks, measuring cups, and bowls.

"Sure," Connie said, slightly confused as to why Rex was in the kitchen. She cleared aside some of the mess. "Have you been enjoying your visit?"

"Oh, yeah, yeah." Rex nodded, crossing his legs and clasping his hands together. "It's great to be back and to see all of the excitement and pure passion for music."

Connie took a seat at the table across from Rex. Maybe he was here to talk about Mitchie, she thought excitedly. "You know, Mitchie, my daughter, loves it here. She agreed to work with me in the kitchen just so she could come."

"Really?" said Rex, obviously impressed by Mitchie's dedication and work ethic. "I saw her perform last night with Shane at the jam. She's talented."

"Oh, I know, Rex," Connie said, leaning across the table. "You should see how much Mitchie loves music! She spends all her time writing songs, and she's really just found her voice this summer. She's learning how to be herself and to share her gift. And *you*—how exciting that you're here? I mean, how often does a teenager get the chance to meet a huge record producer on a search for his next big—"

"Actually," Rex said, cutting her off before she could go any further, "Mitchie is great, Connie. Really. But that's not why I'm here. I'm here to see you."

The color rose in Connie's cheeks, and she sat back in her chair in amazement. "Me?" she repeated. "Why?"

"The next big star I'm looking for isn't a singer; it's a caterer for my annual Labor Day party in the Hamptons." He laughed as confusion swept across Connie's face. "Connie, are you okay?"

"Yes, of course. I just thought . . . I just didn't think . . ." she stammered.

"My usual chef backed out on me at the last minute. It's a huge job—everyone in the industry will be there. I need someone I can trust; someone who will bring something fresh to the table, so to speak."

"Fresh?" repeated Connie.

"Yes." Rex nodded. "I think that person might be you. Brown hasn't stopped raving about Connie's Catering since you came to Camp Rock. And now that I have tasted the food myself, I can understand why."

"Rex," Connie said, composing herself, "that's so kind of you—really, I'm flattered— but I'm just not sure I'm that kind of caterer."

"What kind of caterer?" he asked.

"Well, you know . . . a caterer to the stars!" she exclaimed, throwing up her hands.

Rex laughed. "What do you think you're doing here, then? You're *already* catering to the stars—or future stars, at least. No, Connie, I think you're *just* what I'm looking for."

Connie was speechless.

"What can I do to convince you?" Rex asked.

"Labor Day?" asked Connie. "That's so soon, and I've been away from home all summer . . . I don't know what to say."

"Well," Rex said, slipping a business card out of his pocket and sliding it across the table, "say you'll think about it."

Connie picked up the card. "Okay," she said. "I'll think about it."

"Great," said Rex, standing to leave. "I'm afraid I'll need to know before I leave after the Song Showcase tomorrow. I have Wolfgang on hold, and he *hates* to be kept hanging."

As Rex turned to go, the door swung open,

revealing a breathless Mitchie. "Sorry, Mo—" Mitchie started, but stopped short when she saw Rex. "Hi, Rex," she said.

"Hey, Mitchie. Great job last night."

Mitchie blushed. "Thanks," she said, looking elatedly at her mom.

"See you later," Rex said. "Connie, please do think about my offer," he added before slipping out the door.

"What was that about?" Mitchie asked, confused.

"Can you talk as you whisk?" her mother asked, gesturing to the cartons of eggs waiting for Mitchie on the counter.

"Sure," said Mitchie, quickly opening a carton and cracking eggs into a big ceramic bowl. "Spill it."

In the Vibe Cabin, the girls were avoiding the heat of the afternoon with a new batch of gossip magazines. Ella lay on her stomach on her bed, her feet flopping in the air and a magazine inches from her face.

"Omigosh!" she shouted suddenly.

"What?" Lorraine gasped, looking up from her own magazine.

"Jordan Davids and Alyssa Sharp broke up!" Ella cried, as crushed as if she were talking about her two best friends. "They were *so* cute together. I really thought it would last."

"I didn't," Tess said matter-of-factly. "No one can stand Alyssa. People call her fish face behind her back."

"That's awful." Ella frowned.

Tess shrugged. "That's the biz." She sighed. "Love it or leave it, T.J. always says."

The cabin grew silent again as the girls became reabsorbed in their respective magazines. For a few minutes, the only sound was the flipping of pages. "Omigosh!" Ella exclaimed again.

Tess started. "Jeez, Ella! Stop doing that! What is it this time?"

Ella sat up on her bed. "This," she said, turning the magazine page outward so Lorraine, Peggy, and Tess could see. Below a large picture of Shane was a headline that read: HAS SHANE GRAY FOUND MORE THAN HIS SOUND AT CAMP ROCK?

"Let me see that," said Tess, springing from her bed and snatching the magazine out of Ella's hands. She studied it hungrily, examining the shots of Shane—and one of Mitchie!

"Wow!" Peggy cried, reading over Tess's shoulder. "That's a pic of Mitchie from Final Jam! It says everyone is trying to find out who she is! Wild!"

As she scanned the short article, Tess's face grew pale. This was unacceptable! "How does Mitchie Torres get into a celebrity magazine?" she asked when she was done reading. "She's not even famous!"

Ella considered this. "No, but Shane is, and—"

"And what?" sniped Tess. "The magazine is called *Celeb Weekly*, not *Random Girl Weekly*. It's a disgrace." She sat on her bed, fuming. "*I* should be the one with my photo in that magazine," she said. "That's exactly the kind of publicity I need to take my career to the next level."

What career? Peggy wanted to ask. It wasn't called, *Daughter of a Celeb Weekly*, either, but she kept her mouth shut. She knew Tess well enough to know that when she was like this, there was no talking to her.

"Well," Lorraine said softly, "Jordan's free now. . . ."

"Hmm, I'm interested in where you're going with this," Tess said.

"I'm just saying if all it takes to get in a magazine," Lorraine continued, "is to be seen with a rock star, maybe your mom could set up a meeting between you and Jordan?"

"*That*, Lorraine, is a brilliant idea," said Tess. "I could so easily become the newest

'It' girl," she added. After all, if Mitchie could get in a magazine, how hard could it be?

Back in the kitchen, Mitchie couldn't believe her ears. "Mom!" she whined, the quiches now releasing a mouthwatering smell from the oven. "How could you *not* take the job?"

"How *could* I?" countered Connie as she wiped off the kitchen counters with a sponge. "I haven't been home all summer, Mitchie. Your poor dad probably thinks I've abandoned him!"

"What will a few more days do?" Mitchie argued. "Dad will understand. He has enough of your frozen casseroles in the freezer to last him through New Year's! This could be your big opportunity to take Connie's Catering to the next level. Do you know all the huge music stars who are going to be there? I'm sure that everyone who's anyone is invited, Mom. And all those people could be raving about *your* cooking."

Connie wiped some crumbs from the counter into her palm and sighed. "Mitchie, Connie's Catering isn't exactly set up to go to the so-called "next level." It's a huge job, and I'm just not sure that we could pull it off by ourselves."

Mitchie looked impatiently at her mother. "Then we can hire some more help!"

"There's also the issue of school, Mitchie. You have to be back the day after Labor Day."

"And I will be," Mitchie promised, holding up two fingers in the Scout's honor sign.

Connie pursed her lips for a second as she examined her daughter quietly. "Mitchie, why are you so intent on going to Rex Riley's party? I thought Shane really disliked him."

"He does," Mitchie said. A wave of guilt washed over her and her argument suddenly deflated.

Maybe Mom is right, she thought sadly.

Accepting Rex's offer might royally mess things up between Shane and I. He forgave me for keeping the news of Rex's visit from him, but will this be too much? Does wanting to go to Rex's party mean betraying Shane?

Connie sighed, seeing Mitchie's now sullen face. She untied the apron from her waist and hung it on the hook next to the door. "I'll *think* about it, Mitchie. But don't get your hopes up."

CHAPTER NINE

On the sandy shore by the docks, Caitlyn had set up an improvised "office." She sat on a wooden bench with her laptop in front of her. Next to her, a propped-up, hand-lettered sign read:

GELLAR REACTION
MUSIC PRODUCTION,
MIXING, AND MASTERING

Word that Caitlyn was offering her services for the showcase had traveled quickly, and already a line of campers who were determined to get Rex to notice them was forming.

"So here's the deal," Caitlyn said matter-of-factly to Colby, who was looking for some backup instrumentals for his new song. "I will help you develop and mix the perfect instrumental track—we may have to change a few chords—*if you*, in return, promise to give me a shout-out for my work at the showcase. I need Rex to notice me just as much as you do."

Colby cocked his head, his green eyes thoughtful. It wasn't too much to ask, really. "Okay," he answered. "When do you want me to mention you?"

"Before, during, or after—doesn't matter, but if you do all three, I'll throw in some extra musical fireworks at the end. Maybe some sampling?"

"Deal," Colby said, sticking out his hand to shake on it.

"Great. Meet me at the recording studio at three, sharp," Caitlyn insisted. "Next!" Caitlyn called out and was surprised to see who sauntered over. It was Tess, with her hands behind her back and a big, fake grin on her face.

"Hey, Caitlyn!" Tess said cheerily. "What's up?"

Caitlyn eyed Tess somewhat suspiciously. "Not much. Just conducting some business. Is that what you're here for?"

"Kind of. Well, yes," Tess said. "I need you—I mean, I was *hoping* you would help me with my showcase backing track."

"You're in the right place," Caitlyn said, pointing to the sign. "What did you have in mind?"

"Well, Lorraine—I mean, I . . . we—wrote the song as a ballad, but now I'm thinking we need something with a little more pop, maybe more of a backbeat?"

Caitlyn nodded, listening as she clacked

away at the keys on her computer. "Like this?" she asked, turning her laptop so Tess could hear the sample of music Caitlyn had in mind.

Tess lightly tapped her hand on her thigh in rhythm with the music. When it ended, she smiled. "Exactly," she said.

"You know the price?" Caitlyn asked. She raised an eyebrow, wondering if Tess would be willing to give anyone but herself credit for her performance.

"I have to mention your name," answered Tess.

"Onstage," Caitlyn specified. As she said this, Shane and Mitchie, who had been out in one of the canoes, walked past the line of campers queued up at Caitlyn's makeshift office.

"Hey," Mitchie said, greeting Caitlyn and Tess. Mitchie squinted to read Caitlyn's sign. "Gellar Reaction?"

"That's correct," said Caitlyn. "The only

way I'm going to get Rex to notice me and give me an internship is with some serious viral marketing. So I'm doing some pro bono work in exchange for the exposure. Everyone who uses my sound has to mention me."

Mitchie nodded, impressed with Caitlyn's plan. But Shane scoffed. "Why do you want to intern for Rex Riley?" he asked, sounding offended by the idea.

"Because he's the best," Caitlyn said, surprised that the answer wasn't already obvious.

Shane bristled visibly in disagreement.

Standing next to him, Mitchie felt her heart begin to race. The conversation she had had earlier with her mom was still fresh in her mind. Rex had offered up an opportunity of a lifetime and not once had he been mean—at least not that she'd seen.

But judging by the look on Shane's face, the man was pure evil. Mitchie was confused.

Turning, Mitchie looked Shane right in the

eye. "Caitlyn's right. Why *wouldn't* she want to intern for the best?" she asked Shane. "I know you two don't exactly get along, but he's good at what he does. And maybe he's not as bad a guy as you've pegged him."

Shane shrugged, unconvinced. "Maybe. Or he could be worse."

Mitchie was losing her patience. Shane was being so unresponsive. "Well, he's been perfectly nice to my mom and me," she responded. "He even asked her to cater his big Labor Day party in the Hamptons."

Caitlyn's eyes grew wide with envy as Tess's narrowed. "Seriously?" Caitlyn asked, blown away. "He wants you and Connie to cater the Labor Day party? Do you know how huge a deal that is?!"

"I do now," Mitchie said. "But my mom wants to turn him down."

"Sounds to me like she's making the right decision," Shane observed.

"Shane—" Mitchie began.

"If Rex is a great guy," Shane interrupted, his own patience breaking, "then why did Jordan totally lose himself and his sound when he signed with him? Why did Rex take a cool guy and turn him into a spoiled pop star who ditches his friends?"

Caitlyn's and Tess's heads snapped back and forth between Mitchie and Shane, watching the argument unfold like a tennis match.

Mitchie's hands went to her hips. "Didn't we talk about this?" she asked. "Didn't *someone* just recently find his own voice again?" Realizing that she sounded angry, Mitchie immediately backed off.

"Shane," she went on, softer this time, "even the best people can get caught up in the 'game' sometimes. Everything worked out for you. Maybe you lost Jordan's friendship, but you got your own record deal and career, too. And that was despite anything Rex may or may not have done. Maybe it's time to let the past be in the past and support someone else in what could be an amazing future."

Mitchie reached for Shane's hand, but he backed away. "Maybe *you're* getting caught up in the game," he said before turning his back and walking away.

As Mitchie watched him go, her heart grew heavy. Why was this so hard?

CHAPTER TEN

The night of the Song Showcase was picture-perfect. Tiki torches surrounded the stage by the lake, the reflection of their orange flames dancing on the surface of the still water. On the stage, in a round pool of yellow light from a single spotlight, stood a lone microphone. Strung across the bottom of the stage was a banner that read SONG SHOWCASE.

Anticipation hung heavy in the air as Brown took the stage. It was heightened by the fact that Nate and Jason had come back to see the big performances. They stood in the front row next to Shane. Brown tapped on the microphone, which emitted a shriek of eardrum-piercing feedback.

"Sorry, dude," Sander called from the soundboard. He quickly adjusted some dials.

Brown started speaking into the microphone, hesitantly at first. Then, realizing the mike was okay, his voice grew louder. "As you know," he teased, cocking an eyebrow at the campers who had mercilessly followed him and Rex around for the last few days, "we have a special guest with us tonight."

Every head in the audience swiveled to see Rex, smiling and waving from the back of the crowd. He was standing with Dee and Connie, who had ducked out of the kitchen in order to catch Mitchie's act.

Mitchie was not concentrating on her

upcoming performance at all. Instead, as the others began to take the stage, her mind was stuck on yesterday's argument with Shane. She was miserable and starting to wonder how a visit from a man she barely knew could change things between her and Shane so quickly. Maybe Rex *was* trouble, she reflected, thinking back on how great her friendship with Shane had been just before the executive's arrival. Now, less than seventy-two hours later, Mitchie and Shane weren't speaking.

The only good thing to come out of this whole mess was a song that Mitchie had scribbled in her notebook that day. She had been floating in one of the canoes on the lake and brooding over the recent turn of events. The song had just come to her. She called it "Standing Up," and she had decided to sing it that night.

At least if I'm miserable, Mitchie figured, I can channel my emotions creatively. Plus, this might be the only way I'll get Shane to see my side of the story. We've always communicated best through music.

Shaking off her dark thoughts, Mitchie forced her focus back to the stage. One of the campers was wrapping up a ballad. Slinging her guitar over her shoulder, the girl smiled out at Rex. "Thank you! And I'd like to thank Caitlyn Gellar for her work on this song. Caitlyn, you rock!"

The crowd applauded, and Caitlyn swung her head around to see if Rex had acknowledged the not-so-discreet plug.

Dee climbed onstage to announce the next singer. She checked the clipboard that never left her side. "Next up,"—she beamed, incurably cheerful at all times—"Mitchie Torres!" Tucking the clipboard under her arm, she clapped wildly and exited the stage.

Mitchie took a deep breath, concentrating all of her emotion in the center of her chest. When her heartbeat slowed enough that she didn't fear she'd faint, Mitchie walked to center stage. The crowd grew silent as she adjusted the microphone.

"Hi," Mitchie said, smiling shyly. No matter how many times she performed, Mitchie still got butterflies in her stomach. She nodded at Barron to press PLAY and begin the instrumental backup Caitlyn had worked up for her. As the music drifted into the night, she glanced at Shane. His arms were crossed defensively over his chest and he wouldn't meet her gaze. Sighing, Mitchie released everything that was in her. She closed her eyes to feel the song as she dove into the chorus.

"Stand up for me, and I'll stand up for you," she sang in a clear, high voice. *"When we're on the same team, there's not a loser in this game. When we support each other, it's not about the fame. Stand up for me, and I'll stand up for you."*

As her words floated on the music, the

audience grew steadily quieter. Soon, the only sound that could be heard echoing across the lake was Mitchie's voice. The air that just moments ago had been thick with competition relaxed, and the campers nodded their heads. Connie smiled proudly as Rex listened intently. Even Tess, standing in the front row, seemed to be softening, letting go of her own anxiety about performing for Rex and instead really listening to someone else's song.

Yet still, Shane stood with his arms crossed, apparently unmoved.

As Mitchie drew out the last plaintive note, she finally looked up. The audience exploded in applause. But Shane, the one person whose reaction she really wanted to see, was nowhere to be found. He had slipped away. Smiling sadly, she took a quick bow and left the stage.

Coming down the stairs, Mitchie saw her mother and Tess, who was waiting to go on.

"Great job," said Tess with surprising sincerity as she passed Mitchie to take the stage.

Mitchie smiled. "Break a leg, Tess." Then she turned to her mom.

"Mitchie, that was beautiful," Connie said.

"Thanks," Mitchie said with a sigh. "But I don't think everyone thought so."

"Well, I did. I'm so proud of you. And I can't tell you how much it's meant to me that you've been willing to spend so much of your Camp Rock summer in the kitchen with me."

Mitchie laughed. "I can't tell you how much it's meant to me that *you've* spent your whole summer in the kitchen so that I could *come* to Camp Rock!"

"As you said, 'When we're on the same team, there's not a loser in this game.'" Connie smiled, quoting her daughter's song. "Which is why your father and I talked about it last night, and we both think I should take Rex's catering job."

Mitchie lit up. "Seriously?!" she asked, jumping up and down.

"Seriously . . . but there's one hitch, according to Rex."

"What's that?" Mitchie asked, worried.

"The entire meal has to be red, white, and blue!"

"Blue potato salad it is then," Mitchie said with a laugh. Then suddenly the excitement in her eyes clouded over. "How am I going to tell Shane?" she wondered. "He wasn't exactly thrilled when I told him. In fact, he was the opposite of thrilled. He thinks I'd be working at his mortal enemy's Labor Day bash. We ended up getting in an argument about it yesterday."

"I see," Connie said, biting her lip the same way Mitchie did when she was contemplating something.

"I just wish there was a way I could be

loyal to him and still help you with your big break," Mitchie said.

Connie wrapped her arm around Mitchie's shoulders, hugging her daughter tight. "You know, honey, if Shane really cares about you, he won't make you choose."

Mitchie nodded unhappily. Her mom was right, she knew, but it didn't make the truth any easier to take.

CHAPTER
ELEVEN

With a little help from Caitlyn's spectacular musical stylings, the Song Showcase was a raging success. There wasn't a performer in the lineup who didn't sing or play their heart out.

Brown once again took the stage to bring the night's performances to a close and make one last announcement. He waited for the campers to calm down after the final performance—a reggae/hip-hop piece sung by Lola and backed by Barron on his new bongo drums—before speaking.

"I couldn't be more proud of you guys," Brown said, raising a cheer from the crowd. "Really, I think Rex was hugely impressed."

From the side of the stage, Rex gave an exaggerated nod confirming this. Then he stepped forward to take the microphone from Brown.

"I was, Brown. I really was. But although I thoroughly enjoyed the performances tonight, I have to be honest." Rex paced the stage, microphone in hand. "I'm not here to sign any new talent."

A disappointed murmur rippled through the crowd as Rex continued. "I know Brown told you *I* was your special guest this evening . . . but he lied. I'm really not all that special," he joked. "The guest I'm here to announce is much more special than I could ever be."

The campers looked at each other quizzically. Had they missed something? Was Rex talking about Nate and Jason? But they visited camp all the time. . . .

"Come on out here, guys," shouted Rex, "and let's let Camp Rock be the first to know what's goin' on!"

From the shadows emerged two figures, and as they came into the light, everyone gasped. It was Jordan Davids and Shane Gray—together, on the same stage, and not throwing punches! The girls in the audience began screaming in disbelief and jumping up and down. This was more than a surprise—it was a cosmic event!

Jordan and Shane both smiled graciously next to Rex as the screaming continued.

"Okay, okay." Rex laughed, obviously pleased at the reaction he had gotten. "We appreciate your enthusiasm, but we do have an announcement to make."

Rex passed the microphone to Jordan, and the audience—including Mitchie, who was watching, silent and baffled—held its collective breath.

"I've always wanted to work professionally with Shane, since we were friends at Camp Rock. Now it looks like I will finally get my chance," Jordan said, glancing back at a quiet Shane. "With Rex's urging, I've asked, and Shane has agreed to do a song with me."

The ruckus that ensued after Jordan said this made the previous cheering look like a tea party. People were clapping and hooting and hollering and banging on anything they could find to make noise.

The only one not making noise was Mitchie. Stunned speechless, she weaved her way through the riotous crowd toward the steps, where Shane was just coming off the stage.

"Shane!" she called, and he turned.

"Hi there," he said, coming closer. The hard look that she had seen in his eyes last night was gone. "I'm sorry I didn't tell you earlier," Shane said. "Jordan flew in today to ask me in person. Apparently when Rex saw you and I sing, it got him thinking that I might be up for a duet. So, he asked Jordan, and here we are. I had to run it by the guys and the label first."

"And you said yes just like that?" she asked, crinkling her brow in confusion.

"Not at first, no," Shane admitted. "I wouldn't even talk to him. Then I thought about what you'd said, about leaving the past in the past. I don't want to hold on to those crazy feelings anymore. Jordan and I spent two hours hashing it out. Turns out he's been blaming me this whole time for not keeping in touch with him. He thought I was jealous when Rex signed him instead of me. Then we spent another two hours just jamming like we used to and working up songs. It was awesome. When I realized how much we'd both grown as musicians over the years and how cool it would be to work together, I couldn't say no."

As a smile of relief spread over Mitchie's face, Jordan and Rex came off the stage.

Jordan slapped Shane on the back. "You gonna introduce me to your 'new interest'?" Jordan said warmly, referencing the tabloid headline.

Shane's cheeks turned red. "Thanks, buddy," he said, returning the gentle slap on the back. "I could always count on you to embarrass me. This is Mitchie."

"Jordan Davids." Jordan rocked back and forth on his heels with a satisfied grin.

Mitchie couldn't believe it. Was this seriously her life? Was she really being introduced to Jordan Davids by Shane Gray?

"Um, hey. Nice to meet me," Mitchie stammered.

Jordan laughed. "It certainly is."

Now it was Rex's turn to pipe up. "Shane, I'm glad you've decided to work with us," he said sincerely. "I know the tabloids wouldn't have you believe it, but I really do dig your work and think you have massive talent. I'm excited to see what you and Jordan can do once you join forces."

Shane bowed his head in modesty. "Thank you, Rex. And I think I owe you an apology for holding a grudge all this time. I just missed my friend, I guess."

"No worries," assured Rex, his phone ringing again. "It's the industry, man." He smiled as he flipped the phone open. "Rex Riley," he answered in his smooth, record-exec voice.

"Oh!" Jordan said suddenly. "That reminds me. You guys have got to come to Rex's Labor Day party in the Hamptons, man. It's, like, the biggest bash in the industry! Everyone will be there—Diddy, Beyoncé, Justin, man!" Even Jordan sounded starstruck by the invite list.

"Did I hear someone say Diddy?" a female voice interjected. It was Tess, who just

111

happened to be wandering by. "My mom sang backup on an album he did. It was so sweet. Oh, excuse me," she said suddenly, turning to Jordan. "How rude of me! I don't think we've met yet. I'm Tess Tyler."

As she stuck out her hand, Tess smiled. Jordan shook it and smiled back. Shane glanced at Mitchie, who was desperately trying to stifle a giggle.

"Jordan," said Shane, trying to pry Jordan's and Tess's eyes apart, "why don't you stay for a while and catch up? You don't have to get back to L.A. tonight, do you?"

"That's a great idea!" blurted Tess before Jordan could answer.

Jordan glanced at Tess and then Shane. "Yeah, why not? We've got a lot to catch up on, after all."

"Sorry to interrupt," Rex interjected, returning from his business call, "but that was the label. They've decided on three backup vocalists. They want them to be female, so they don't compete too much with your voices. What do you think?"

"I think great," said Shane.

"Yeah, man," Jordan agreed enthusiastically.

"Excellent," Rex said. "We can cover the details at my party. Mitchie, you'll be there helping your mom, right?"

Mitchie nodded, and Shane looked confused. "Wait. What?" he asked.

Nervously Mitchie turned to Shane. "My mom decided to take the gig catering the Labor Day party. It's a huge opportunity, and she'll need someone who knows the ropes to help her. . . ." She waited for Shane to look upset. It didn't take long.

"No, no, no," he said, and her face fell. Rex and Shane had just buried the hatchet; certainly that meant he wouldn't be upset if she worked Rex's party?

"Why not?" Mitchie asked.

"Because your mom's going to have to find

another assistant. You're going to the Labor Day party as my date," he said.

Mitchie beamed.

"Yeah, man! Great idea," said Jordan. He turned to Tess. "What are you doing over Labor Day weekend? Think you could take pity on a dateless pop star and pencil me in for that Saturday night?"

For a moment, Tess was speechless, and Mitchie had to restrain another giggle. Finally she said, "I'll have to check with my publicist, but I think I can arrange to be free." Tess turned to Mitchie. "It'll be a double date!"

"Great!" Mitchie said, trying to sound sincere. It was going to be a very interesting party.

Humphrey loaded Rex's Gucci suitcases into the trunk of the limo as Rex and Brown said good-bye. Turning, Rex looked wistfully back at the Camp Rock landscape spread out before him under the summer moon.

"You know, I really do envy these kids, Brown. They have their whole lives before them. That reminds me—there's a camper who must have slipped me her production demo at some point, a girl named . . ."

"Caitlyn?" asked Humphrey, who couldn't help but overhear.

"Exactly," said Rex, squinting at Humphrey curiously and wondering how his limo driver had read his mind. "Caitlyn Gellar, I think."

"Sure!" said Brown. "Caitlyn's talented, always in the production booth or on that laptop of hers."

"Will you do me a favor?" asked Rex.

"Oh, the big shot record exec wants me, the lowly camp director, to do *him* a favor?" asked Brown.

Rex chuckled. "Just tell her to send me her resumé when she graduates high school. I think Sweet Jam might have a place for a kid like that."

"Will do," said Brown, opening the door for Rex, who slid into the car's plush, black leather interior.

"See you on Labor Day?" asked Rex.

"See you on Labor Day," confirmed Brown, closing the limo door. As he did, he could hear the sound of Rex's cell phone going off yet again. As the limo drove off down the road and faded into the distance, leaving only the sound of crickets, Brown smiled. He was happy to be at Camp Rock and not in the back of a limo.

"So," said Tess, intertwining her arm in Jordan's, "who else is gonna be at the party?"

"Let's see . . . John Mayer, Celine Dion, Mariah Carey . . . But you probably already know all these people through your mom," Jordan added.

"Right. Of course," said Tess, waving her hand dismissively, as if the prospect of sipping iced tea with the biggest music stars on the planet was nothing more than an average Saturday afternoon. Tess guided Jordan toward the mess hall, leaving Shane and Mitchie to follow.

"Oh, boy," Shane whispered. "Jordan always did have an eye for the wild ones."

"That's fine," Mitchie said, giving Shane a sly smile. "I hear you have an eye for the mysterious ones."

Shane let out a laugh and Mitchie smiled. Second Session was officially rocking!

Going Platinum

By Helen Perelman

Based on "Camp Rock," Written by Karin Gist & Regina Hicks and Julie Brown & Paul Brown

"Aloha! And welcome to the luau!" Brown Cesario cried. The director of Camp Rock stood on the stage in front of the lake, the summer sun setting behind him. Many of the campers were wearing grass skirts, and everyone wore a brightly colored plastic lei around their neck. Brown beamed as he inspected the crowd. Satisfied that everyone looked the part, he jumped off the stage. He had work to do.

"Boy, Brown is taking this pretty seriously, huh?" Mitchie Torres said to her friend, Caitlyn Gellar. The two were sitting on one of the beaches near the stage. "He's like a little kid at Halloween!" She eyed Brown's bright pink and yellow Hawaiian shirt as he danced over to the food table.

"Brown does love a good theme night," Caitlyn said, grinning. "Last year he wore a Frankenstein's monster costume for the Monster Mash. He painted his whole face green. He looked awesome!"

Mitchie smiled. Unlike Caitlyn, who had been lucky enough to come to camp before, this was Mitchie's first summer at Camp Rock. But she already knew that Brown was wild enough to do something like dress up as a large green monster. She still couldn't believe she was here! She was so thankful that her mom had gotten the job as the camp cook. Mitchie could never have come otherwise. And that meant she might not have ever met Caitlyn, Shane Gray, and all her other friends. To Mitchie, helping her mom in the kitchen was a small price to pay.

"Mmm," Barron James declared as he walked over to the girls. "This is some good coconut-pineapple chicken." He was with his best friend and music partner, Sander Loya. Together they had a soulful sound that was always a hit at any jam session. "I am so grooving on this dinner!"

"And I'm so getting more!" Sander said, heading back over to the food table.

Mitchie smiled. She had helped her mom prepare all the food. Connie took pride in selecting a menu that fit each of Brown's theme nights.

"Isn't this great?" Lola Scott asked, coming to stand between Mitchie and Caitlyn. She had a flower in her curly brown hair and a pink lei around her neck. "I love the tiki torches. It really feels tropical around here tonight." She sang a few lines from a Bob Marley song for effect.

Caitlyn nodded. Lola's voice was always so strong and confident—and on pitch. As Mitchie and Caitlyn stood up, she started to sing. The three friends made their way over to where Brown was dancing.

"Check out Brown's moves!" Lola said. "He's a real hula superstar!"

The girls watched Brown dance with Dee La Duke, their musical director. A circle had formed around the dancing duo.

Across the circle, Mitchie saw Tess Tyler. The camp diva was in a shell-shaped bikini top and a *real* grass skirt. No way would she wear a plastic one, Mitchie mused as she watched Tess sway to the beat. At Tess's side, as always, were Lorraine Burgess and Ella. Lorraine had quickly become a part of Tess's entourage. She had even moved into the Vibe Cabin after Mitchie had moved out.

Suddenly, Peggy Dupree jumped into the circle to dance with Dee. Mitchie smiled to see her friend having so much fun. After Final Jam, Peggy had walked away from being one of Tess's backup singers. Peggy had used her full name—Margaret Dupree— when she performed at the jam, and she had taken first place. Peggy still lived in the Vibe Cabin and occasionally sang with Tess, but she had grown closer to Mitchie and Caitlyn.

The dancing continued as Dee pulled Shane into the circle. Mitchie giggled. Shane was a guest instructor and the resident star of Camp Rock. He was also the lead singer of Connect Three, a band that was steadily climbing the pop charts. Mitchie laughed as she watched Shane try to hula. His cheeks flushed red under his thick, dark hair. But he looked relaxed—and not at all like a pretentious rock star.

That hadn't always been true. Earlier in the year, Shane had thrown a fit about a wrong coffee order on a photo shoot. The incident had made all the magazine headlines. Shane's label had sent him to Camp Rock to mellow out for the summer. Not only was Brown his uncle, but the camp was where he had gotten together with Jason and Nate, his Connect Three bandmates. Shane hadn't wanted to duck out of the A-list scene for the summer, but the hiatus had served him well. The press on Connect Three was once again more about their music than about the spoiled behavior of their lead singer. And Shane had really started to get back to his roots, partly by working as a guest instructor and partly because he had started hanging out with Mitchie.

As Shane moved his hips from side to side the way Dee demonstrated, he caught

Mitchie's eye. "C'mon, Mitchie," he called. He flashed her one of his million-dollar smiles. "Let's see you move!"

Performing in front of a crowd was still hard for Mitchie. She was better at singing alone in her cabin or composing music. Writing songs was what she loved most. But slowly she was getting more comfortable singing in front of people. But dancing the hula? Now that was a different story!

As she got the rhythm, Mitchie began to smile. That was the good thing about Camp Rock—everyday was a new experience! She couldn't wait to see what was next.